I0579035

A Thief In The House

A Stella Madison Caper

Lilly Maytree

LIGHTSMITH PUBLISHERS
Thorne Bay, Alaska

ISBN: 978-1-944798-45-1

Published in the United States by
Lightsmith Publishers
P.O. Box 19293
Thorne Bay, Alaska 99919

Website: www.LightsmithPublishers.com

Cover photography by Steve and Becky Brown

Lightsmith Publishers is an imprint of the Wilderness School Institute, a non-profit educational organization that offers outdoor youth activities in wilderness settings, including training in wilderness skills and nature studies, as well as the publication of curriculum on related subjects, through the Wilderness School Press, and their children's imprint Summers Island Press.

A Thief In The House / Lightsmith Publishers Edition / Paperback

*To my dear friends everywhere. Those
past, those present...and the ones
I have yet to meet.*

"A true friend... advises justly, assists readily, adventures boldly, takes all patiently, defends courageously, and continues a friend unchangeably."

William Penn

1

Stella Madison felt as if she had walked into a fortune. Considering her new apartment cost less than half what her other one did (and had nearly twice the space), there was even enough left over in her budget to loosen her belt a little. After all these years! For the first few weeks she was in heaven. To be honest, it wasn't really what one would call an apartment, but to Stella, it was even better.

It had charm – Old World charm – and if there was anything she loved more than books, it was places that even remotely resembled days gone by. True, the "Villa" had definitely seen better days. A rambling old mansion overlooking southern California's sea in one of the city's oldest sections. Even in this economy, the place would cost millions if put on the market, in spite of the fact it hadn't been properly cared for in years.

The landlady was a likable, middle-aged widow named, Millie, who sported a bountiful figure and a head of thick auburn hair without a speck of gray in it. Always done up in a rather sixties-fashion French twist. Stella felt an immediate kinship with Millie. While her ramshackle renovations had turned the once-stately mansion into a hodge-podge of individual living quarters, each had its own unique flavor.

It was hard choosing between the third floor rooms with a balcony but no outside entrance, or, the ground level suite next to the main kitchen that had French doors which led right out into a garden. In the end she picked the upstairs because of the delicious quiet, and that adorable private balcony she could enjoy in her pajamas (if she had a mind to) and watch the many moods of the distant sea.

Besides that, the Colonel was only two doors away.

His set of rooms occupied the same floor on the south end and included a converted attic that made for vaulted ceilings and slanted windows. Two of which opened onto the roof. Out there he had placed a patio table with chairs, and innumerable clay pots full of all manner of growing things. It was obvious that this was mostly where his incredible tan came from.

One could see the swimming pool from there, along with a Greek statue (some woman named Phoebe with one arm broken off and the other holding a pitcher), but there had been no water in the pool for years. Too much work to maintain, Millie said, though when her husband was alive there were parties nearly every weekend during the summer. Movie people drove all the way up from Hollywood just to escape the sweltering heat.

Now, parties of any kind were rare and the Villa's "guests" consisted mostly of a few regular tenants. Each possessed some oddity that had endeared them to Millie, and none of them were wealthy. Counting Stella and the Colonel, there were six, along with three others who dropped by for meals. There was a retired carpenter, a bank teller, a teacher (some cousin of Millie's who had retired early on disability), and even a senator. Stella later discovered the senator to be only eight months old and the illegitimate son of the bank teller, who felt he might fare better in life with a more respectable name.

In coming to the Villa, Stella hadn't just moved into a new home but a new family. Something she hadn't had in years. A rather odd one, to be sure, but a type of family nevertheless. With all her new-found friends to help out, the dreaded task of moving actually turned into somewhat of an adventure. Which is why when the second crisis struck it didn't send her into as much of an emotional loop as the first one had. Thank heaven. Because that sort of stress isn't good for anyone, much less a woman in her sixties.

It happened on a Thursday.

While Stella was staring intently into her bathroom mirror, carefully applying a thin line of schoolroom glue to her upper lip before pressing on a false white mustache. Suddenly, a blood-curdling scream that echoed all the way up to her third floor apartment, stopped her cold before she could even get it on straight. For a moment she froze. What in the world? Without another thought, she flew out the door and down the two long flights of stairs, across the main foyer and along the hall, through the dining room and into the large kitchen. An exertion which completely winded her.

Mason (the retired carpenter) was already there, filling a glass with water at the sink, and Millie (the landlady) was sobbing into a napkin at the huge oak-veneered table that had replaced a stunning mahogany classic just last week. She had some kind of letter in her hand and had obviously received bad news.

"What is it, Mil?" Stella panted as she sank into the chair next to her. "One of your kids?"

"No, it's—"

"What kind of get-up is that?" Mason cast a critical eye at Stella's slightly cocked mustache and slicked back white hair (that was normally fluffy and neatly tucked under) as he handed Millie the glass. "Always the quiet ones!"

"Oh, I – good heavens!" Stella gasped and tried to pull the pillow she had tied around her middle up over her lacy undershirt. "It's a costume. I'm actually going on, tonight. Hand me your shirt, will you, Mase? I thought somebody was dying or–"

"My shirt – get your own shirt – for crying out–"

"Give her your shirt," Millie sniffed, "She needs to rest a minute before going all that way back up. Then finish reading this, Mason. I'm too upset to do it!"

Mason sluffed off the plaid flannel that was hanging unbuttoned over his sleeveless white tee-shirt and tossed it over the table to Stella in a waft of manly odor. He picked up the letter, ran a hand through his close-cropped salt-and-pepper hair, cleared his throat, and began to read.

"Dear Mr. Palmer... Mister... don't they know he's been dead for two years?"

"Oh–I'll explain later!" Millie snapped.

"Dear Mr. Palmer,

This is to inform you that the estate of Ethan J. Willoughby will be sold at auction on June 17, and the proceeds divided among his heirs. Be advised that a representative of the law firm of Castle, Todd, and Boone, will arrive at the property on May 10 to check the inventory against his records.

If all is in order, you will be given a letter of recommendation for future employment along with a check in the sum of one thousand dollars to assist you in relocating, as stipulated in the will.   On behalf of the Willoughby family, we would like to thank you for your many years of service as caretaker of the Villa Nofre.

Sincerely,

S. T. Boone, Esq.

Attorney at Law"

For a moment there was a dead silence, during which a cloud of disappointment descended over Stella like a gathering storm.

She had so been enjoying herself here! Not to mention that another move would completely deplete her resources, again. But while Stella was feeling stormy, the two people across from her were approaching hurricane proportions.

"Holy–gee, Mildred!" Mason leapt to his feet so fast his chair clattered backward onto the floor. "Are you crazy or just stupid!"

"I'm sure Millie feels bad enough already, Mason," Stella admonished. "There's no need to rub it in."

"I've got to calm down and think over my options!" Millie blew her nose one last time and tucked the napkin into a pocket of her flowered, over-the-head apron. "Right now, I don't know what I'm going to do!"

"Your only option is to turn yourself over to the police or skip town, you crazy– BOOM! His fist came down on the table so loud Millie clutched her heart and Stella squealed as he continued to thunder. "Why didn't you tell me you didn't own this place!"

"I was going to." Millie retrieved the napkin and began dabbing at her nose again.

"When? Over a year ago when I started busting out walls to turn it into apartments, or last summer, when you had me sell off that five thousand dollar Chelini Venus statue to finish remodeling!"

"Five thousand dollars!" Stella gasped.

"You knew I was short of money, Mason – you've always known that. How..." Millie looked up at him. "Just how much would it take for you to get things back to original condition?"

"What? Are you out of your – it takes a lot more to build something up than bust it down, Mildred. Even if you had it, you couldn't do it for any five thousand dollars. Or even fifty!" He rubbed a hand over the two-day growth of stubble on his chin and sighed miserably. "By the hoagie –– somebody could go to jail for this – and it isn't going to be me!"

With that, he reached for the old Greek fisherman's cap that hung on a peg by the back door, plopped it on his head, stomped out, and slammed the door after him with a bang.

"Jail!" Stella gasped again.

"I need my nitro–" Millie moaned, still clutching at her heart. "If I try to get up I'll faint!"

Stella hurried to rummage in the spice cabinet a few moments and found the bottle.

"Oh–" Millie held her breath for a moment until a new pain subsided. "I can just imagine what you're thinking about me, right now. But you don't know what it's like to be left all alone–all alone without even enough money to pay the electric bill!"

"Oh, but I do," Stella soothed as she shook one of the tablets into the woman's trembling hand.

"I never considered it stealing." Millie popped the pill in her mouth and rambled on.

"It was all going back into the place. E.J. kept sending me cryptic letters that said – rely on you. Rely on you! He should have known I couldn't be relied on! Then he didn't answer anymore, at all. I had all these people to take care of, and one thing just led to another. Now I can't even think straight!"

"Maybe we should ask God to intervene," Stella offered. "He was a great help to me during my murder investigation. To tell you the truth, going to jail, at my age, probably would have landed me in another mental institution."

"What?"

"Oh, don't worry," she replied quickly to the shocked expression. Imagine! All these years and the secret had slipped out as easily as talking about dinner! She certainly hadn't meant to do that. "It was sort of a mistake, actually." She tried to explain. "The only way I could escape–"

"You escaped?" Millie's eyes widened in

horror and she swallowed her pill instead of letting it dissolve.

"Heavens no! Why it's practically impossible to get out of those places once they put you in. What I meant was–"

There was a loud rap on the wall next to the stove.

"Let Gerald out of the dumbwaiter, will you, Stel?" Millie dropped her auburn crowned head into her hands. "I don't have the strength!"

"What I meant to say was..." Stella went to the sliding metal shutters built into the wall and heaved them apart. "The Colonel happened along just at the right time to help me out. And I didn't even know him back then. Why it was... it was just like a miracle!" She reached through the ropes and took hold of the tall lanky form of Millie's cousin, who was practically doubled over in the small space.

"Oh thank you – I don't believe we've

met – why, Stella, is that you?"

"Of course it's me. I'm going on tonight because Lester Boyles came down with the flu. Actor's pay instead of understudy."

"What's wrong with Millie?" He smoothed back the thinning brown hair that had fallen forward during his descent and started toward the table. "Millie, did you know I just saw Mason headed downtown in his undershirt? What's the matter with him? And I heard a scream like bloody murder right in the middle of my–"

"I'm in trouble, Gerry," Millie mumbled. "We all are!"

"What?"

"Going to take a miracle to get us out of it!"

"What kind of trouble?" He righted the overturned chair and then sat down in it.

"Let's just say you better start looking for another place to live."

"E-gads – I can't afford anywhere else!"

He chuckled uncomfortably and cast a searching eye toward Stella for reassurance. "She's kidding, right?"

"I'm not kidding." Millie got hesitantly to her feet, and retrieved a bottle of brandy from above the stove.

"Are you sure you should be mixing that with your medication?" Stella worried.

"I need to brace up! You might be right about the Colonel though. He does have a way of making things come to right."

"Well, I didn't mean the Colonel so much as I meant, God. The Colonel just happened to be the person He sent along."

"Like I said, he has good connections. Especially with Mason too mad at me to count on. Maybe you could bring it up, Stella, on account of you have a better influence over him."

"Over God? Why, I wouldn't even presume!"

"I meant the Colonel. He'll do anything

for you. Will you ask him?"

"Well, if you think I should. But what exactly should I ask?"

"I say," Gerald grimaced until the space between his two front teeth appeared beneath his meticulously trimmed mustache. "Millie hasn't made me pay a dime since before Christmas. Why can't I just go wherever you go, Mil?"

"You'd look awfully silly in a women's prison, Gerald," his cousin replied.

"E-gads!" He threw Stella another pleading look. "She's kidding, isn't she?"

"I'm not kidding." Millie fell heavily back into her chair, thumped down a juice glass, and poured till it nearly overflowed. "Here's to a miracle... a big one!"

2

Meeting the Colonel had elevated Stella's lifestyle to new heights. In a few short weeks she had gone from solitary days of meals alone in front of the evening news, an occasional day out for shopping, and the majority of her hours spent with books and the Internet. Not that she hadn't been content. But the fact was she had accepted the belief that this was "normal" for women of her age, and that there was absolutely nothing wrong with one's closest physical relationship being the family doctor.

Upsetting this balance had brought about

a crisis... or rather it had seemed like one, at first. True, her brief job at the library had not been what one would call successful. But it had changed something in her. It showed her that she was still capable of actually doing something in life (instead of just talking or reminiscing about it) and that one's physical resources were renewable. Even at her age! Now, she found herself quite incapable of going back to the old ways. She had far too much energy. Along with a newly developed taste for the good things in life. Things like being responsible for whatever "comes under your eye" and hollering help (up to heaven) if you needed it.

If Stella had known someone would actually respond when you hollered for help, she wouldn't have waited until she was a senior to do it. But, no matter, she knew it now. The odd thing was, that along with the help she had personally received during her own catastrophe, came an intense desire to help others. What's more, it was the act of helping others that gave her such a high sense of energy. In fact, she was almost sure of it. As if God, Himself, were actually replenishing any resources she expended on His behalf. A rather absurd perspective, really, and she certainly wouldn't admit it to anyone. But she felt that way, just the same.

And it was the Colonel who had introduced all these things to her. He said now that she had become partners with God, His part of the bargain would be to see that things began working for, instead of against, her all the time. Imagine that! The fact that things had immediately begun working out better than they had in years turned Stella into an enthusiastic believer. Not only had she been snatched from a frying pan into a paradise, the Lord had miraculously landed her another job, besides.

It had happened on a Friday, while waiting for the results of Ms. Thatcher's autopsy. The Colonel had taken her out to an off-beat mystery dinner theater on the corner of South Twenty-third and Main to get her mind off things. In truth, it was neither a theater nor a restaurant. The plays (all mysteries) were what were commonly known as the off-Broadway variety. The food was made up of the most common of already-prepared entrees that came out of boxes and cans. Still, it had atmosphere.

Ensconced in an old renovated cannery, it was supported by a flock of consistent patrons that had kept it solvent for nearly thirty years. Not only did her first experience succeed in taking her mind off that horrible investigation (of which she was acquitted), but it was there that she learned of the opening for the "victim's understudy." It paid twenty-five dollars per performance, or a whopping sum of one hundred, should one actually have to perform. Considering the fact that performances were only held on

Friday and Saturday nights at seven, as well as two o'clock on Sunday afternoons... it was enough (linked with such a reduced rent) for her not to even miss her paycheck from the library.

Now Lester Boyles had the flu, and for the first time in the month and a half she had been employed, she was actually going on. As a victim, she only had eight lines and was killed off halfway through the first scene. She had planned on devoting the entire afternoon to perfecting her costume – an old gentleman with a hearing disorder – and getting herself into character.

That is, until Millie's catastrophe erupted.

Now she barely made it on time to rush onto stage at her cue, deliver a somewhat stilted eight lines, and keel over dead as a blank shot rang out and the house lights went black. The company could let her go for such a poor performance. But the very thought that she was – once again – being thrown out (along with all Millie's other boarders) back into that sea of high cost for the most basic of living standards... managed to greatly overshadow her acting debut.

Still, the Colonel met her backstage with flowers for her first performance, and whisked her off to a secluded little Italian place for a late snack afterward. The fact that she could not remove the false mustache without considerable pain to her upper lip made her decide to go in costume and work on the problem after she got home. Thus it was that Stella got her first proposal in twenty years while she was impersonating a man.

It started out simple enough.

"Have you been home, yet, Oliver?" She tried to think of a way to bring up the situation of losing their homes to Millie's advantage.

"Only to change clothes before I came to meet you at the theater." He brushed at a few bread crumbs that had fallen onto the wide front of his blue pressed shirt. "Strange doings going on there."

"Oh?"

"There was old Gerald laying prostrate on the couch with an ice-pack on his head, and a heat-pad on his liver. Babysitting the Senator while Lou Edna went to interview for a night job. Humph! Gone on another date if you ask me. That girl is always lying about one thing or another."

"You're humphing again," Stella informed him. "Where was Millie?"

"That's another thing. According to Gerald..."

A waiter appeared with an ice bucket and a chilled bottle of champagne. The young man couldn't have been far past his twenties, but he withdrew the bottle, dried it off with a small towel, and expertly held the label out for the Colonel to approve before opening.

"What's all this?" Stella asked amazed. "I

thought we were–"

"Bit of a special occasion," he replied with a warm and sudden smile.

"I would hardly call a mediocre delivery of eight lines the beginnings of a theatrical career." But she only objected half-heartedly. On the inside, there was an answering warmth beginning to spread all through her. "It's the most wonderful thought, though, Oliver. Absolutely wonderful!"

"Not the career. Although you died admirably, my dear, and I think you really could go somewhere in the field if you truly enjoyed it." He lifted his glass in signal for her to do likewise as the waiter discretely retreated.

Stella raised her glass.

"It's for you, Stella Madison – my charming and adorable friend – in hopes that you might do me the honor of sharing the rest of your life with me."

"Why, Oliver!" she gasped. "Is this – is

this–"

"It is," he beamed. "Here's to you, my dear."

What else could she do but drink?

"Well? Don't leave me in suspense, Stel. What do you say?"

"I say... I say you're certainly the best friend I ever had in my whole life, too, Oliver, and under any other circumstance..."

His gray eyes grew wide with surprise and he slowly set down his glass. "What circumstance? I was so certain you would–"

"Oh, I would, I would! There isn't anything I'd like better. Honestly! But Oliver, I would hate like anything if you thought you had to marry me just to rescue me out of another bad circumstance."

"Another bad circumstance... what's happened, now?"

"You didn't talk to Millie?"

"What's Millie got to do with anything? She can't object to the way we've been spending so much time together, she's been chumming around with Mason for years. She's not one of those stuffy types, if that's what you're worried about."

"Oh, I'm not worried about that. Besides, I couldn't have stayed away from you even if she had been."

Another warm smile from him, and she realized he had just elicited one of her deepest secrets from her. How is it he kept doing that? "But–you didn't actually talk to her?" She picked up her glass again, drank two quick swallows, and hoped that lighting was low enough to let the rising flush of her face go unnoticed.

"Not hardly. Gerald told me she'd locked herself in her room since three o'clock, Mason was down at the docks in his underwear getting royally plastered for some reason, and if I wanted anymore details I had to get them from you after you died!"

"Oh." She felt a cold wetness soak onto

her upper lip and run down her chin. "Good heavens–I forgot about the mustache!" She searched for her napkin but it wasn't there, so the Colonel handed her his. "Thank you." She pressed it against the offending thing and felt it come loose: but only on one side. "Uh-oh!"

"I have an idea." He slid his large bulk around the horseshoe-shaped booth to her side of the table, touched a corner of the napkin into the saucer of spiced oil that was for dipping their fresh bread in, and put a hand under her chin while he dabbed gently at the glue. In a few moments the mustache was off.

"Thank you, again." Stella wrapped the drooping piece of white fur in the napkin and tucked it into the pocket of her suit jacket. "In case Lester still feels unable to go on tomorrow," she explained. Then she caught the eye of a woman at the table across from them. Suddenly, it seemed everyone in the place was looking. "Oliver – people are staring at us!"

"Two old gentlemen making a scene, I shouldn't doubt it." He chuckled and moved back to his own side. "Good thing I didn't kiss you!"

"I should say!"

"Now, what's this about bad circumstances?"

"It isn't just me, it's all of us. The whole Villa family."

"What?'

"It seems that our un-stuffy Millie has been illegally pilfering estate funds for almost two years, by selling off valuable artifacts that never even belonged to her in the first place."

"You're kidding."

"I wish. The truth is, she'll be found out in a few weeks, when they come to take inventory, and we are – all of us, even Gerald –out of our lovely place to live! And as for

Mason..."

She pushed on in spite of the colonel's suddenly shocked expression, "He's worried he will be charged as an accomplice, since it was him that punched out all the walls and did most of the actual selling of things."

Which didn't exactly exude the delicacy she had promised Millie to use.

But the bad news was finally delivered.

3

There was an unofficial meeting, next morning, in the kitchen. By the time Millie came down, Stella and the Colonel had already fixed breakfast, and Gerald was counting out his medications to be taken before meals.

"Good morning, Mildred." The Colonel set a fresh cup of coffee in front of their disheveled landlady (her pink terry robe was buttoned crooked and she hadn't even bothered to fix her hair). He got right to the point as Stella retrieved another plate and more silverware. "I understand there is a crisis at hand. For all of us."

"Mine's more serious than yours." Millie's tone was abnormally sarcastic. "On account of I probably won't get to pick where I live." She heaped two spoons of sugar and poured cream until her cup nearly overflowed.

"No need to jump to conclusions." He picked up her plate long enough to whisk two pieces of French toast off the grill along with some bacon. "We haven't put our heads together, yet."

"I'm sure we'll come up with something," encouraged Stella.

"The only thing I can come up with," said Gerald, "is I'll probably end up on welfare. E-gads! At least Millie let me keep my dignity."

"Thank you, Gerald," replied Millie. "I've spent nearly the whole night trying to figure it out and can only see one way open to me."

"What's that?" Stella poured a bit more coffee into the Colonel's cup as he sat down and then turned the fire off under the grill.

"To run."

"But you can't do that," she objected, "it would make things ten times worse for you when you're caught. And they have amazing ways of catching people these days, too."

"Have you considered talking to the people, first?" The Colonel took a swallow of his coffee without taking his eyes off Millie over the rim of his cup. "Considering the heirs are already wealthy, they might not be interested in the property so much as the sale of it. People like that usually want things done as quickly and cleanly as possible. They might not even care about your renovations."

"You think?" For the first time, Millie's face brightened as she looked up from her plate.

"Stranger things have happened. Even if they did care... well, they've left you on your own for so long, it might not matter so much. Add the fact they think they're dealing with your husband and you might even get off scott free."

"I never thought of that!" she dropped her fork and stared at the Colonel with a sort of awe. "I never did!"

"Then, again, they might be the vindictive sort and decide to press for maximum charges."

Millie's face crumpled into dismay as quickly as it had brightened. "Oh, God help me!"

Stella breathed a sigh of relief at the saving words, and saw the hint of a twinkle come into the Colonel's eyes as he took another contemplative swallow from his cup before answering. "Yes, indeed. Besides that, as Stella pointed out, it's no easy thing becoming a ghost, these days."

"E-gads, man!" Gerald practically choked on his last pill. "Are you suggesting Millie kill herself?"

"Certainly not."

"I considered it," Millie admitted. "Only I wanted to decide when I was stone cold sober to make sure it was the right thing."

"Millie!" Stella was shocked. "Killing yourself is never the right thing!"

"Oh, I know. I know." She slumped low in her chair and thoughtlessly moved a bite of French toast back and forth across a puddle of syrup. "It's just that Mason left–without even looking back!"

"He'll be back," predicted the Colonel in a comforting tone. "Mase is just hot-headed, you know that. Why I'd be willing to bet he's been wrestling the problem around, himself, all night somewhere and–"

There was a sudden noise of high heels beating their way down the marble foyer like the rapid fire of artillery, and the group at the table looked up in time to see the swinging mahogany doors burst open from the formal dining room. It was Lou Edna, blonde shoulder-length hair overly permed, dressed up in a too-short skirt, and a too-low blouse that sported the same shocking color as her too-red lips.

"Somebody help me!" she panted as she hefted the beautiful curly-haired boy farther up on her slender hip and dropped an over-stuffed diaper bag onto an empty chair. "I can't take him to daycare today – he's got trench mouth!"

"Trench mouth –" Stella cast horrified eyes on the smiling, good-natured child. "How ever could that happen?"

"Oh, here –" Millie slid her chair back and reached out for him. "Come to Auntie, luv, and we'll take care of it."

"But shouldn't he see a doctor?" Stella worried.

There was a screech of breaks out on the road as the young woman handed the boy over. "Bye, baby," she pressed her cheek to his and made the sounds of a kiss so her lipstick wouldn't smudge. "Be a good boy and feel better! Thanks, Mil."

"Don't mention it."

She was out the kitchen door in a whirl and left a swirl of too-strong gardenias descending on the rest of them while the Senator began jabbering to himself and tugging contentedly at Millie's buttons.

"He doesn't seem sick," observed Stella.

"He's perfectly fine," said the Colonel. "She just can't afford daycare on the weekends. I really don't know why she has to carry on such a charade with all these exotic diseases when we all know perfectly well–"

"Morning, Pop!" They heard her voice echo back to them from halfway down the walkway and all fell into an immediate silence to listen.

"Hello, Shortcake," Mason mumbled as she passed.

"He's back!" Millie quickly redid the clip that was only halfway holding up her hair. "Oh, I'm a mess!"

Gerald got up to open the door and peer down the walkway. "You don't look half as bad as him, Mil, he's still in his undershirt. Hello, Mason! Just in time for breakfast, old man!"

"I ate already," He pushed past to hang up his hat before squaring off to the group at the table. "Wooden nickels! Except for Henry, here, you're all a bunch of nincompoops that couldn't take care of yourselves even if–"

"I beg your pardon!" Stella interrupted. "For your information, I – for one – have been taking care of myself for years."

"And this coming from the queen of burly-que!"

"Here, now, Mason," the Colonel came quickly to her defense. "One can hardly call what Stella does down at the mystery theater the least form of burlesque."

"You should have been here yesterday, then, when she was prancing around in her Victorian secrets."

The Colonel's mouth fell open and he turned toward his fiancee to implore in a hushed whisper, "Stella, is that true?"

"Not the way he says it," she replied.

"Mason Jefferies!" Millie got to her feet, shifted the dark-haired toddler expertly onto an ample hip, and squared off for a battle. "If we're all nincompoops, it speaks little enough of you for hanging around us for so long! You're attached to every one of us here and you know it."

"I don't know any such thing." Then he pointed a finger at her for emphasis. "There isn't a one of you I couldn't walk away from right now and never–"

The Senator reached toward the outstretched finger with a squeal of delight and a gurgle of, "Pop! Pop-pop!" To which Mason involuntarily responded with an answering grin as he took the child from Millie.

"Go ahead–leave then–if you feel that

way," Millie challenged.

"Well.." He sat down in one of the chairs like a deflated balloon and sighed heavily. "I said I could. Didn't say I was going to."

"E-gads, Mason!" Gerald thoughtlessly began counting out his morning medications, all over again. "Do you – I say, do you have to give us all such a case of the nerves when we're worried enough, already? Are you in or out?"

"I agree with Gerald," said the Colonel. "Seems we've got some risky business ahead of us any way you look at it. So, if there are any reservations..."

"Reservations," Mason muttered. "I been up all night wishing I had more reservations."

"Can we take that to mean you've come up with some sort of plan?" The Colonel moved his chair closer to the table and looked intently at his grizzled friend. "You're the real genius among us when it comes to strategies, Mason. I'm sure everyone will agree on that."

"Oh, I got a plan all right... but I wouldn't exactly call it genius."

4

Stella could sense danger in every aspect of her being but she ignored it. Because at the same time, she also felt a thrilling since of adventure such as she had never experienced before. A clear case of mixed emotions, obviously. So she sat quietly and sipped at her Moroccan Mint tea while she listened to the Colonel go on about the details.

She loved the smooth comforting sound of his deep voice (he really could have been a radio announcer if he hadn't opted for a career in the military), and let her gaze drift out over her balcony to the twinkling lights of boats in the harbor. It was a balmy evening, unusually warm for spring, but there was a scent of rain in the air that would probably lead to one of those violent spring storms.

"Of course you can't see it from here," the Colonel went on. Even so, he pointed off to the left as if she could. "It's moored out in the bay, just beyond the fishing fleet."

"It's quite the fantastic plan, Oliver... do you really think it will work?"

"I do." Then he laughed to himself as if the mere thought brought him pleasure all over, again. "Leave it to Mason to come up with such a scheme!" He drifted into his own thoughts for a moment and Stella noticed how his curly gray hair shown like molten stone in the moonlight and gave him the look of some distinguished Greek philosopher. "If nothing else, it ought to be a rollicking good adventure. The sort I haven't had for years! Hope to heaven I'm still up to such things. More importantly, I hope Stuart is still up to them. He hasn't had that boat out any farther than the horizon since he retired."

"For heaven sake, do you think he'll even be able to manage such a long voyage? And Alaska! How in the world did Mason ever come to own property up there? A lodge of all things– where we could all stay together!"

"Won the deed in one of his weekly card games when a former service buddy came through. I wouldn't get too excited about the word lodge, though, Stel. From what I hear, it could be anything from a dilapidated hunter's shack to a deserted hotel. He's never even seen the place."

"Then he's always intended to go there?"

"Not that I know of. I think he was saving it back more for trading off in another game if he had to. That sort of thing. The only real adventuring Mason's ever done was a stint in the Navy about thirty years ago. But our steps are ordered, my girl, are they not?

The Lord knew we would all need such a place, about now, if we wanted to stay together."

"What if he's right, though? Because – Oliver – as much as I disagree with Mason on most things, I'm afraid he's right about the capabilities of all the rest of us."

The Colonel laughed out loud at the idea (Stella loved his laugh– so spontaneous and engaging). "I admit it could turn into a regular nightmare!"

She cast him a scrutinizing stare over her tea. "Are you having second thoughts then?"

"Not on your life. If it's one thing I've learned over the years it's never to pass up an opportunity to really live! That's one of the secrets to longevity. To..." he fished for the words, "drink up life with everything you've got! How about you?"

"Oh, I like drinking up life, too," she replied quickly. Not that she had thought so much about it before now.

"Having second thoughts, I mean. Because if you're feeling the least bit hesitant, my dear, we don't have to go. We could settle ourselves in some modest little apartment and live like ordinary people."

"But we're not ordinary." Stella returned to the chaise lounge with her tea and sighed deliciously at the strains of classical music she could faintly hear coming from inside. "It would be too hard to give up this kind of living, now I've had a taste of it. I'd want to help them even if I couldn't go. They certainly helped me out when I needed a place to live. And such a lovely place, too! I don't mind saying I'll miss it terribly, Oliver."

"I'll miss it, too, of course." He pushed out his lower lip and took a deep breath, as if preparing to do a particularly hard thing. "I've flourished here. In terms of my career, that is. It's where I came up with the idea for my *magnum opus*."

"Your great work?"

He looked at her with unmasked admiration. "So few people even know what that means, these days, Stella, I'm truly impressed."

"Of course I know what that means. I taught school for over twenty years, dear. English lit, mostly."

"I keep forgetting that. How are you at copy editing?"

"One of my strong points."

"Ah, signs of the divine, again. I've got ideas enough to live longer than Noah, but my grammar... well, now that's another thing. Isn't it just like God to give me a partner who can really help? We were destined to be together!"

A shimmer of thrill ran through her. "Oh, I feel the same way, I really do! It's like I've been locked up in a cocoon for simply years. Now all of a sudden, everything is so vivid and intense. Why, it's... it's like I was half dead, and I've come alive, again!"

"My own feelings exactly. After all, that's what the term 'born again' is really all about. Without it, one barely feels a fraction of the mere excitement of living."

"Born again..." Stella took a sip of her tea. "Such an odd way of looking at things if you ask me. Still... if it's one thing I know for certain, the only thing I could look forward to a couple of months ago, was ending up in a decent rest home. And, now, I'm on the verge of going to Alaska! Who would have thought?"

A delighted chuckle escaped him. "A surprise from God, I'd call it. Wrapped up just for us!"

"Exactly! I'm amazed at how much I've come to care about all these Villa people, too. And in so short a time! Why, they feel like family. Do you know I lived the better part of ten years with most of the same neighbors in my old apartment building and never felt like this toward any of them? Isn't that strange!"

"One sees everything differently after being born again. Especially friendships. It's because not until then can you truly love, Stella. *'A friend loves at all times,'* as the Bible says, and that's something that makes you even closer than family. The kind of friend that *'sticks closer than a brother.'* He left staring out at the fishing fleet and came to sit down in the lounge across from her. "Even for such a rag-tag bunch of misfits as ourselves–there's no qualifications to it. But I'm amazed you took to it all so easily, I really am."

"I'd say it was you who had a hand in that." She smiled her most charming smile. "I really think I wouldn't care where I lived, as long as you were there."

"Listen here, Stel." He sprang to his feet again. "What do you say we pay a visit to the county courthouse before the big adventure gets started, and make things official. We could even–" Two bars of From *The Halls of Montezuma* suddenly emanated from his shirt pocket, and he paused to fish out his cell phone. "Henry, here. They're back with the charts already? All right. The north wing den. Right."

He closed the phone and returned it to his pocket. "Captain Stuart will be calling our first planning session to order in five minutes," he answered to Stella's questioning gaze. "Let's not keep him waiting."

"But, my goodness, Oliver, you can't just drop a question like that and then–"

"Oh, I'm not dropping it." He helped her to her feet. "On the contrary, my dear, I'm saving it for later. We'll come back up here after the meeting and–"

Now there was a rap at the inside door and Gerald's voice rang out, "I say, Henry, are you in there?"

"How is it Gerald can get himself into the

dumbwaiter all right..." Stella set her half-finished tea on the kitchenette counter as they passed through her lovely little sitting room on their way to the door. "But he can never get himself out?"

"Just wooden cabinets for openings up here. But the ones down in the kitchen are those blasted heavy metal things that are on self-shutting springs." He opened the door for her.

Such manners! There was hardly anything she enjoyed more.

"I say, old man," Gerald was still standing there. "Would you mind stopping by the kitchen on your way past?"

"Be glad to," the Colonel replied as they split off to opposite ends of the old hall.

"I think he'd feel a lot better if he walked up and down instead of riding," Stella whispered.

"You 'd have a hard time convincing him." Then he laughed. "I'll tell you one thing, though. There aren't going to be any dumbwaiters to ride up and down on the *Dreadnaught*!"

Another shimmer of apprehension went down Stella's spine. "What a foreboding name! Why it doesn't give me any sense of strength or security at all."

"You think that's foreboding, wait till you meet Captain Stuart."

5

Somewhere during the next hour, the rain came. But Stella hardly noticed it because of her eagerness to catch a look at this "Captain" who had volunteered to take them all to Alaska in his "*Dreadnaught*." Not to mention the pleasantly crackling blaze in the the floor-to-ceiling stone fireplace that Mason had started in the cozy, north-wing den where they were all gathered.

Stella loved open fires and was delighted when the Colonel steered her over toward a set of comfortable cushions on the hearth, that bordered either side. "Captain

Stuart" was already there when they came in. To say he didn't exactly fit Stella's idea of a captain, was an understatement.

"All right..." A faint smell of diesel fuel wafted up from the coffee table as the gray-bearded man–dressed in a moth-eaten fisherman's sweater and a pair of threadbare jeans–unrolled an old yellowed chart and weighed down each end with a dessert plate. "Here we are right here."

He pointed to some obscure spot at one end of the paper and ran a finger along the coastline all the way up to the other. Then he unrolled another chart from a pile on the floor, slipped the corners under the plates and repeated the gesture. Finally, in a last dramatic fling, he unrolled yet another and did the same thing before intoning seriously, "that doesn't even get us half there."

"My word," Stella breathed. "All that long way in the *Dreadful*?"

The Captain jumped as if the insult had

been physical and turned a vengeful steely-blue glare from beneath bushy black eyebrows toward the fireplace.

"Look here, Stuart," the Colonel intervened quickly. "We're all aware of how long the trip might be. Just what exactly are you getting at?"

"It's not just a long trip, Henry. What I'm getting at is it's a devil of a long trip around a devil of a lot of treacherous rocks, through a devil of a lot of dangerous currents. Not to mention a devil of a lot of some of the worst unpredictable weather you can find on the planet."

"E-gads!" Gerald gasped.

"You never told us that before, Mason," Millie cast a wary glance toward the carpenter, who was sitting backward in a kitchen chair with his arms crossed over the top as he looked on.

"You want to go where you won't be found, Mildred," he answered, "it's going to be where most people don't go. What's it going to cost that's what I want to know. Not a one of us here – except Shortcake – that isn't trying to eke it out on a fixed income."

"I don't even know if I'll have that anymore," Millie admitted. "I can hardly disappear into thin air and still go on claiming Sam's social security."

"Cost isn't the biggest worry." Captain Stuart began to pace back and forth in front of them like a coach readying his team for a game. It was then Stella noticed he was wearing tennis shoes with no socks: one of which had a hole where a large brown toe was sticking through. "What worries me is if you can even handle it. And seeing as how I don't plan on getting myself accused of negligence for taking you all out there – maybe even get my papers revoked – I figure we better get serious."

"Serious how?" asked the Colonel.

"Serious as in we all meet at six o'clock

tomorrow morning for sea trials."

"Six o'clock?" Stella mentally calculated how much in advance that meant she would have to get up... it was an hour she hadn't seen in years.

"What if the weather's bad?" Gerald worried.

"What if it is – who cares? Better out here in our own bay instead of off in all that devil of an ocean. We'll hit every kind of weather there is before this trip is over, so—"

Lou Edna sauntered into the room in no hurry, wearing a black kimono with an embroidered dragon that started on one side and ended on the other. Her curly blonde hair was wet and she smelled of almond oil with a hint of lemon. Her face was more beautiful without make-up than with and she seemed just as comfortable settling into the brown leather couch and putting her feet up as if she were, by herself, in her own apartment.

"Sorry I'm late," she said to no one in

particular. "The Senator sleeps so much better after a bath, I figured it would be a good night for it." Then she tossed a flowered tube of moisturizing lotion to Gerald at the other end of the couch. "Do you mind Gerry? I've been on my feet all day."

"Of course not," he replied with a good natured smile as he took the cap off and squirted a liberal portion into his hand. "I say, you better get all the foot rubs you can while we're still here."

Her face crumpled into a frown and she bust into tears.

"Why, Lou Edna." Millie got up and quickly sat down between them so she could take the girl into her arms. As if she had been fifteen instead of twenty-two.

"I don't see why I have to be left behind just because I have a baby!"

"But what about that little apartment you've been so excited about? Close to your work, and all. We'll even help with daycare, right Mase?"

"Well..." He rubbed a thoughtless hand over his chin as if trying to fiigure yet another expense into the already escalating budget."

"Besides," Millie went on in a soothing tone, "There might not be any jobs where we're going. And as a mother—"

"But you're the only family we've got and it's—it's desertion!"

"What?" Millie gasped.

"I can't say I blame her." Gerald began to rub the lotion over his own hands and forearms rather than just sit there holding it. "I felt the same way when Millie first told me I'd have to look for another place. Haven't lived by myself in years."

"My boy's too little to know where you all went—he could die of grief!"

"Oh, for heaven sake," muttered the Colonel.

"And he hates daycare! You know he

tries to crawl away from me, now, whenever I say, let's go bye-bye?"

"The poor luv!" Millie mourned.

"Why don't we put it to a vote?" suggestted Stella. Who knew where the child could end up when that girl went off on her tangents?

"Shortcake stays with the family," Mason suddenly replied with such a decisive tone it turned every head in his directtion. "Not that everyone isn't entitled to their opinions. It's just I never left anybody behind who needed help and I can't do it, now."

"Thanks, Pop." Lou Edna pulled away from Millie long enough to snatch a tissue from a decorative box on the end table. "I knew you'd understand. You're the only one who—"

The melodic sound of old-fashioned door chimes interrupted her and Millie clutched Gerald's forearm in a death grip. "Somebody's at the door!"

The Colonel got to his feet. "Probably just—"

"Don't answer it!" warned Millie.

"Calm down, Mildred," Mason said. "Isn't a soul in this city knows what we're up to in here. Go ahead and take a look-see, Henry."

The Colonel moved out with his familiar determined stride, and—as if caught in some weird spell—the rest of them rose from their seats, almost in unison, and followed him down the hallway at a safe distance.

Which is why there was such an audible collective gasp when the door swung open and, almost as if on cue, a rumble of thunder and a flash of lightning revealed the dark silhouette of a slightly-stooped-over man. Who looked to be wearing a trench-coat, and a battered hat with rain pouring down in streams off the brim.

"Deluge," said a hoarse, wheezing voice as the figure stepped inside. "Streets are starting to flood, already."

"By the hoagie," Mason muttered, "It's Mr. Peabody from the antique shop I been dealing with!"

"No," Millie pronounced in a voice tinged with doom, "it's E.J.'s brother... J.D."

"Right" The man pulled off his dripping hat to reveal a shiny bald head above tufts of drenched white hair hanging down over his ears. "On both accounts. How are you doing, Mrs. Palmer? Still making those wonderful lemon meringue pies?"

"Not lately," Millie quavered. "But there's a plate of snicker-doodles in the den."

"Well, there's a first for everything. Thank you, sir," he said as the Colonel helped him off with his coat and hung it on a nearby hall-tree, where a puddle began to form immediately on the marble floor beneath it. "Colonel Oliver P. Henry, I presume? Read your medal of honor book, and enjoyed every bit of it!"

"Good of you to say so," the Colonel flashed him a friendly smile. "There's a fire in the den you can dry out next to. Plenty of coffee, too."

"Splendid. I have a lot to say."

"Do we have to drag things out?" Millie reached for her nitro that she had taken to carrying around in her pocket since the catastrophe began. "If you're going to have me arrested, J.D., I'd appreciate if you just tell me and get it over with."

"I'd appreciate knowing why you been impersonating some antique dealer," Mason countered. "Not to mention I had no idea this crazy dame didn't own the place."

"Mason! You—you deserter!"

"I'm no deserter. And I've done plenty enough other things in my life to hang for, even if I don't deserve this one. Let's get on with it, Peabody."

"Will you sit with me, Stella?" Millie whispered an aside to her as the group flowed back into the den like a receding tide. "You having already been through it, and all."

"I'd be honored, Mil," Stella took up the position at her side. "That's what friends are for!"

Considering the gravity of the situation, it was only natural for the man to be given the best chair: a recliner of soft Italian leather that flanked the fireplace. A spot usually reserved for Gerald due to his frail condition. Except at the moment, one couldn't have pried him away from Millie's other side.

"Where's Lou?" Millie scanned the room as the three of them sank down onto the couch. "She was here a minute ago. I think she's upset."

"Took off like a rabbit at the first sign of trouble," the Colonel huffed as he returned to his seat by the fire.

"Girl's got a fine sixth sense." The Captain gathered up his charts without re-rolling them, and headed, by habit, toward the back door through the kitchen. "See you all in the morning."

"If I could only look forward to it!" Millie's voice had gone quavery, again, and Stella grasped her hand in a supportive squeeze. A gesture which gave the distraught landlady the courage to venture, "Any chance you'd agree to payments till everything's paid back, J.D.?"

"You'd have to live to a hundred and fifty, Mildred." Mason straddled his chair, again, and scratched thoughtfully at the three-day stubble on his chin. "But maybe if I was to kick in some of my--"

The imposing figure in the chair raised his hand in a signal for silence as he took a moment to wash down a bit of snicker-doodle with a swallow of strong coffee. At which point every eye in the room was on him with strained anticipation. "The time has come," he began, "for..."

Millie fumbled for her nitro, again, and dropped it.

"Some long overdue confessions." An expression of sadness passed over the wrinkled face and he heaved a great sigh. "This whole situation has been weighing heavily on me since my brother's passing and I want to straighten things out."

"I'd be willing to sell my car, too," Millie offered. "And—believe me—if there was any way in the world to get back all those things..."

"No need, Mrs. Palmer. You see, those things never left the family in the first place."

"What?"

"Because E.J.—poor businessman that he was—would have driven us to the poorhouse if we hadn't come up with some means of reigning in such wild extravagance and all those crazy ideas of his. That bumbling Hollywood film company was the last straw."

"I knew he had to be losing money on that," she admitted. "Every movie he made was a flop."

"Precisely. Then there was the number of ex-wives he had piling up to support. At any rate, I had a false will drawn up, making him believe this villa was his sole inheritance from our father, in spite of the fact he was the oldest, and should have had the controlling hand in managing the business side of everything."

He paused for another heavy sigh and took another bite of his cookie. "But he was such an engaging fellow it didn't seem to matter to him. Ran through all his money in no time. So, the next project he came asking a loan for—I believe it was to finance that epic monstrosity THE CURSE OF EGYPT."

"That one was the best," Millie conceded. "If you were to pick the least rotten out of a batch of bad eggs."

"It was an embarrassment!" said J.D. "My own wife, who happened to be E.J.'s third ex..."

"No kidding!" Millie marveled.

"Yes, the one with a starring role in it—first and last, I might add—threatened to divorce me if one more poop-a-raz-zee plastered another picture of her in front of everyone's dinner tables. Well, I was between a rock and a hard place with the two people I cared most about."

There was another long moment of excruciating silence, during which the only sound was the soft clump of one of the logs burning through in the fireplace. Stella noticed none of them dared break the old man's spell for fear of which way he might turn. After all, he held the power to let Millie and Mason loose into glorious freedom, or bind them with chains. Figuratively speaking.

"That's when I came up with the idea of the antique business. Sort of an 'if-you-can't-beat-'em,-join-'em' type deal. Because I knew he was about to sell off every valuable thing he had. *Peabody's Peculiar Treasures*, was simply my way of continuing to loan money to E.J., and get back my wife's expensive belongings he wouldn't let loose of, at the same time. Especially the art collection."

Millie tightened her grip on Stella's hand and whispered, "The art was the first thing I let go!"

"Hold on," Stella whispered back, "I think I see daylight ahead!"

"I had no idea E.J. left you all destitute for so long until we were notified of his plane accident in Madrid."

"He died in a plane crash? No wonder I stopped hearing from him!"

"Of his injuries, eventually. Never recovered enough to make the long trip home, even with the best care. He did have some pleasure in the fact that he never totally lost the *Villa Nofre,* though. Like it was some kind of accomplishment. But you know he already had more friends than a politician over there? I actually believe..."

He reached for another snicker-doodle from the plate on the hearth beside him, and stared into the fire a moment as if seeing something. "I believe I envied him just then. Especially with my old wife grouching around that museum of a beachfront place we live in, wanting to know why the poop-a-raz-zee never take her picture anymore, and why can't we be like E.J. And travel the world? I don't have to tell you how fed up I was with this whole mess!"

"So, where does that leave Mildred and me, Mr. Peabody? You going to press charges, or aren't you?"

"I thought of it."

"My nitro—my nitro!" gasped Millie.

Stella quickly reached down and retrieved the little brown bottle from the floor. She popped the top off, shook one out for Millie, and then another when Gerald held his hand out for one, too.

"But as close as I am to facing eternity, myself, I figured I better make some amends. Truth is, I'm more to blame than either of you, considering it was my idea in the first place. Used Palmer to keep tabs on what E.J. was up to. Then after he died, kept the same thing going with Mason, here."

"How—" Millie practically choked on the words. "How long have you known Sam's been dead?"

"Since I hired a private investigator to find him when two of our most valuable paintings ended up at Christy's Auction in New York, a few months back."

"Now, that, I had nothing to do with!" insisted Mason.

"I told Sam not to take those when he left—"

"Yes, I found that out, too. So, I don't want any arguments from either of you. I've thoroughly considered my final decision. Personally, I've got a lot riding on this. Have to do what's best for everybody all the way around."

As if that explained everything, he got to his feet, and started getting ready to leave. Which gave Stella the fleeting thought there might be a police car waiting outside to arrest the pair. Her heart practically dropped down to her shoes. Along with Millie's medicine that she hadn't put the cap back on, scattering little white pills over the floor when they all stood up with him.

J.D. gathered himself to the fullest height

(as his permanent stoop would allow), bored into Millie's crumpled expression with eyes full of firm resolve, and pronounced, "Reprieved!"

At which point, she dropped back onto the couch in a wave of relief, while a spontaneous cheer erupted from everyone else. Then the old man reached into the inside pocket of his tweed suit jacket and pulled out a long envelope.

"Your thousand dollars," he replied to the astonished woman. "Best of luck in Alaska."

"Alaska," mumbled the Colonel, coming to lend Stella a hand at picking up all the little white pills. "How did you find out about that?"

"Mason gave me a call from some local pub, last night, to say he needed to get out of town fast, was headed all the way up to Alaska, and what would I give for the companion piece to Chilini's Venus."

"Mason, you didn't!" Millie exclaimed.

"I knew we couldn't get out of town on our good looks, Mildred. Desperate means calls for desperate measures. He gave me another five thousand."

"Give it back—this instant!"

"Consider it part of my amends," said J.D. "I actually envy you going on such an adventure, anyway. It's the sort of thing E.J. would do."

"You could ride up with us if you want," Millie offered. "Then fly back from somewhere."

"Appreciate the invitation. But don't worry about me. I plan on making a few lifestyle changes, myself. You see, I sold this entire headache to a friend of mine who's going to tear it down and build a first-class spa and conference center. Property was worth more than the place."

"Probably got a pretty penny for it," mumbled Mason.

"I did, indeed. Another reason I felt

obligated to spread a little of it around."

"But after pilfering your things we really don't deserve it!" insisted Millie.

"My dear lady," he replied as he stashed a few snicker-doodles into his pockets for later. "Who on earth of us ever does?"

"Well, I just can't thank you enough!" Her eyes brimmed with tears and she reached into her pocket for a tissue. "You're a real friend, J.D."

"Words money can't buy, I can tell you that. God help me to live up to them with whatever time I've got left."

At which mention of that wonderful phrase, Stella and the Colonel both stopped picking up pills, looked knowingly at each other... and smiled.

Author's Note

A Society of Friends

William Penn (who was quoted at the beginning of this story) was born into a life of privilege and favor. It was said, *"He was of the 'well-born' in the worthiest sense of the word. For fifteen generations, the best and bravest blood of England had flowed in the veins of his family, unstained by a single act that history should blush to record."* That is an amazing legacy, considering he lived during a very dark and chaotic time in history. One which he described as "times too rough for print."

It was an age when kings were sovereign (whether good, or bad). Common people had little say over their own their lives. During William's teen years, King Charles II decided that everyone should convert to his religion, and all others would be outlawed. Most complied. However, there were many who didn't, and thousands were put into prisons, or executed for their beliefs. The group that "agitated" the king most were the Quakers – or, as they called themselves, the "Society of Friends." They believed in each individual having a personal relationship with God, rather than committing themselves to whichever religion the current royalty happened to belong to.

William Penn landed in prison, many times. In places like the Tower of London, and Newgate, notorious for their filthiness and squalor. From which he once replied to his father (who offered to buy him out of it), "My prison shall be my grave before I will budge a jot: for I owe my conscience to no mortal man." How many of us could do that?

Yet, what impressed me most was the response others had to him. During his most famous trial, after not having been allowed to present evidence for his defense, the jury brought a verdict of "not guilty." Which the judge ordered them to reverse. When they didn't, the entire jury was fined a year's wages, thrown into prison with William Penn, and told they would be "starved unless they changed their verdict."

Two months later, they won their case, and from that time forward, juries were no longer under the rule of the judges, and could not be punished, or coerced for their decisions. Reading this account made me wonder what made people willing to go to such lengths for someone else. But William Penn was a true friend and went even farther for them. He is credited not only with establishing the state of Pennsylvania as a place of refuge for religious freedom, but for developing the very foundational principles that make up our modern democracies of today.

Many of its citizens were bought free from English prisons with his own money. He called it his "holy experiment." A place where people were free to worship as they chose, work in whatever business they wanted, while being tolerant of others at the same time. A government based on friendship and respect. One that worked things out through negotiation rather than by force. He called it Philadelphia: a Roman phrase that means "city of brotherly love." That city later became the birthplace of Benjamin Franklin, and where Thomas Jefferson would eventually draft the Declaration of Independence, and the Constitution. Truly, it became what William Penn had prayed so hard for it to be... "the seeds of a great nation." A place where people were no longer servants, but friends.

About Lilly Maytree...

Lilly Maytree is the author of *Gold Trap, The Pandora Box*, and *The Stella Madison Capers*. Books that sent her careening along on her "Mystery Tours" with her captain husband aboard the *Glory B*. She loves sharing these adventures with readers. It has even been said that she time-travels (but that's probably just a rumor). To find out about her current adventures, simply visit:

LillyMaytree.com

You can get in touch with her via the contact page. It might take a few days if she is adventuring far away... but she always comes back sooner or later.

Other Books By
Lilly Maytree

The Stella Madison Capers...

Home Before Dark
(Caper #1)

Here is the first of the Stella Madison Capers, the story of how everything started, and how she escaped from a catastrophe that seemed to come out of nowhere. Which is the nature of catastrophes but it's so hard to be logical when you're in the middle of one. It's also the story of how she met the colonel (if you're interested in that sort of thing).

A Thief in the House
(Caper #2)

Stella Madison is back, this time with a bevy of friends. But just how far should a person go when it comes to sticking by their friends? There's a thief in the rambling old mansion she moved into. And while it was someone who was quick to lend help when Stella needed it most, how can she possibly return the favor without jeopardizing herself along with them? No person is obligated to go that far... right?

Voyage of the Dreadnaught
collection of 4 Stella Madison Capers
Here is a collection of the four Stella Madison Capers covering the entire voyage of the *Dreadnaught*, through the Inside Passage to Alaska. Includes: **Sea Trials, The Pushover Plot, Lost in the Wilderness**, and **The Last Resort.** Also includes a brief account of Lilly Maytree's true-life voyage along the same route, in the sailboat, *Glory B.*

Novels...

Gold Trap
Megan Jennings is headed to Africa for high adventure and divine appointments until she makes a small wrong turn. But what is faith, if not to strike out against impossible odds believing you will win? Or leap out into the dark knowing someone will be there to catch you? Someone does catch her... but it isn't who she was expecting.

The Pandora Box
Journalist D.J. Parker learns the location of a famous cache of diamonds that were stolen during World War II. What she doesn't know is—the federal government has been following

the case for years. With an old journal to lead the way, she sets out aboard a yacht that once carried the infamous Herman Goering. A thrilling treasure hunt that could either prove to be the adventure of a lifetime... or her worst nightmare.

For Writers...

Unspoken Rules

Popular books (those stories everyone likes no matter what the subject) all have certain things in common. And what they have most in common is what they DON'T do. Within the following pages, dear writer, you will find the three most important "don'ts" of popular fiction that I learned when I was studying the masters. Why? Because I love research and I never mind sharing my notes.

Writing Rules!

(a mysterious student handbook)

A mysterious little desktop handbook that can help anyone (well, almost anyone) with writing rules. Especially if you are a student and have to write things all the time.

For Parents...

Behave Yourself!
Teaching your children to discipline themselves.

Are you tired of bickering during daily routines encroaching on way too much of your family time? Here is a book that offers a two-week program that teaches your children to discipline themselves. Hard to believe? Here are the step-by-step secrets of how it's done, and why it works.

The Nature of Children
(And how to deal with it.)

A manual based on a compilation of parenting articles Lilly wrote over several years as a columnist for Childcare Magazine. It is a result of many requests from parents for more information about that content and the foundation of the methods she used both in raising her own children, and in her classrooms.

After years of experience, she has a lot to say about what motivates children and has implemented many of her unique ideas into books and programs that others can use.

Sea Trials

A Stella Madison Caper

by Lilly Maytree

1

Stella Madison flinched when a cold splash of spray hit her face and she tightened her hold on the bouncing rail. The motorboat was loaded to full capacity, with Colonel Oliver P. Henry's large bulk ensconced precisely in the middle for better balance. She and her friend Millie (who had insisted on wearing a bright orange life preserver) were at the very front, practically hanging over the bow. Gerald and Lou were in the last seat behind the Colonel, while the Captain stood up in the stern with a casual grip on the tiller and the outboard turned up to full throttle. The Senator was riding like a king in a backpack-type apparatus attached to his mother.

"E-gads!" Gerald complained as they bounced off another ripple of chop and sped through the darkness. "I say – is it necessary to go all out?"

"It is if we want to get out of this bay before ten o'clock," answered Captain Stuart, whose gray hair was standing up all over like a wild man in the wind.

It was six thirty-seven in the morning. On a Sunday.

Just as Stella began to wonder what in the world she had let herself in for, Stuart cut the motor to half-power and they spent the next ten minutes weaving in and out around the dark shapes and shadows of other boats anchored across the bay. The sky was still black as night. While her hurried breakfast of donuts and coffee was beginning to churn with a mind of its own, a great ominous wall gradually emerged out of the darkness. The Captain turned the little craft smartly, and cut the motor. He tossed a line over a cleat as they drifted up against a floating wooden platform, and then jumped out to run forward and secure the bow.

"Here we are, mates!" he crowed. "Go easy – one at a time, now – it's too early to have to fish anybody out of the water!"

Stella climbed out and stepped gingerly onto the rocking platform with a distinct sense of vertigo and nothing to hang on to. Just as she began to sink to her knees to keep from falling, she felt Captain Stuart's strong grasp under her arm and he propelled her forward to a dangling metal stairway. It stretched diagonally up against the wall – who cared where it went – as long as it took her away from here. She clutched the cold wet rail and began to climb…

End of excerpt.

To read the rest of this Stella Madison Caper, visit us online at:

Lightsmith Publishers.com

Also available from Ingram
wherever books are sold.

If you enjoyed reading this Lightsmith Publishers **Little Traveling Book**. please share it with someone. You can also find other inspirational stories by visiting:

LigtsmithPublishers.com

If you have children, you may even enjoy browsing the *"mysteriously different books"* over at:

SummersIslandPress.com

Both imprints are divisions of the Wilderness School Institute, a nonprofit educational organization based in Thorne Bay, Alaska, where they *"take learning back to nature."* You can find more information about them here:

WildernessSchoolInstitute.org

Thank you for reading this book! Will you consider writing a review for it at your favorite online bookstore? In the meantime, may you be specially blessed, knowing that you have blessed others simply by reading their stories.